Happy Cat

by Steve Henry

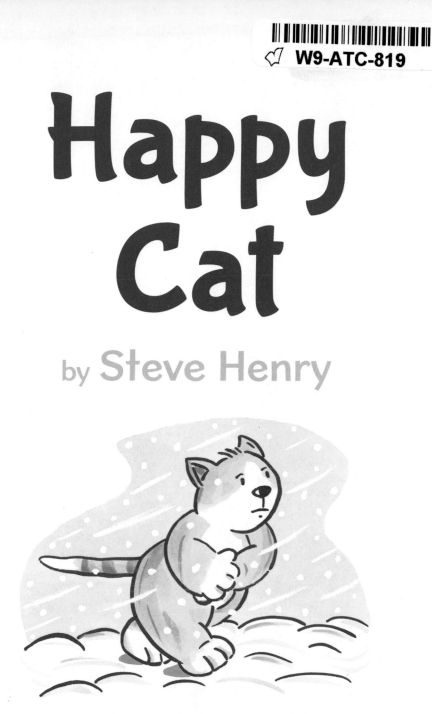

I Like to Read®

HOLIDAY HOUSE • NEW YORK

I Like to Read® books, created by award-winning picture book artists as well as talented newcomers, instill confidence and the joy of reading in new readers.

We want to hear every new reader say, "I like to read!"

Visit our website for flash cards, activities, and more about the series:
www.holidayhouse.com/I-Like-to-Read/
#ILTR
This book has been tested by an educational expert and determined to be a guided reading level B.

I LIKE TO READ is a registered trademark of Holiday House Publishing, Inc.

Copyright © 2013 by Steve Henry
All Rights Reserved
HOLIDAY HOUSE is registered in the U.S. Patent and Trademark Office.
Printed and bound in June 2020 at Hong Kong Graphics and Printing Ltd., China.
The artwork was created with watercolor, gouache, ink, and brown craft paper on Arches Hot Pressed Watercolor Paper.
www.holidayhouse.com
3 5 7 9 10 8 6 4

Library of Congress Cataloging-in-Publication Data
Henry, Steve.
Happy Cat / Steve Henry. — 1st ed.
p. cm. — (I like to read)
ISBN 978-0-8234-2659-1 (hardcover)
[1. Cats—Fiction. 2. Animals—Fiction. 3. Apartment houses—Fiction.] I. Title.
PZ7.H39732Hap 2013
[E]—dc23
2012006579

ISBN 978-0-8234-3879-2 (paperback)

For my parents,
who always let me draw

Cat was cold.

He went in.

Cat met Rat.

Cat went up.

And Cat went up.

Cat met Dog.

Cat met Rabbit.

Cat
went
up.

Cat met Bird.

Cat met
Elephant.

Cat went up.

He went to the top.

Cat was happy.

All were happy.

I Like to Read®

Visit http://www.holidayhouse.com/I-Like-to-Read/ for more about I Like to Read®
books, including flash cards, reproducibles, and the complete list of titles.